THE EPICAL TALES
OF BILLY BUMPKIN

To Kisu,

Enjoy the Stories!

David J Murphy

By David J. Murphy

Dedicated to Fred M. Murphy, the guy who brought us
Billy Bumpkin:

November, 1887 – June, 1979

TABLE OF CONTENTS

Author's Introduction

In pulling this collection of stories together into a cohesive whole, I have passed around early copies to my wife and some respected friends. From what I hear back, there seem to be two questions that are consistent, and I would like to state them and address them here.

The two questions seem to be:

- Who is Billy Bumpkin? What does the narrative cover in these stories?

- What is the intended purpose of these stories? What audience are they written for?

So, I will address the questions one by one.

Who is Billy Bumpkin? What does the narrative cover in these stories?

Billy is a young boy who lives in a small, rural town. His mother is named Betty Bumpkin. In this sequence of stories, Billy progresses from the age of seven to the age of twelve. In the narrative sense, some of these stories have the element of *romance*, but I use this word in its sense from about five hundred years ago. At that time, many stories were written about still earlier ages, going back to the time of quasi-historical characters like King Arthur. Many such legends had their roots in the area of southern Europe, where civilization had sprung from the Roman city state and its language and the offshoots of its language. Hence the name *romances*.

In this type of story, many places and events and experiences would have been familiar to everyday life. However, many of the events and personalities somehow would extend past the realm of everyday, common experience. So, in these stories we have characters like Arthur and Merlin, swords stuck in stone, the Holy Grail, maidens who befriend unicorns, and many other fascinating events and people. These elements of romance make for fantastic storytelling, even down to this day.

My grandfather first told me Billy Bumpkin stories. I was very young, maybe three years old. Our family lived in an apartment in Atlanta. My grandfather was a traveling salesman. He sold candy – primarily chocolate candy. So whenever he came over, he brought us treats. Then he would take us upstairs and put us to bed and tell us his Billy Bumpkin stories. I suspect he made them up on the spot, but the content didn't matter. What mattered was the experience of this wonderful man calmly laughing and telling us these stories while the chocolate put us quickly to sleep.

When I had my own kids of course I told them Billy Bumpkin stories. Then when they started bringing grandchildren into the world, it was time for more of the same. Somewhere in the years I added Betty Bumpkin to the saga.

In recent years, my wife and my kids have asked me to write the stories down so they could be preserved. Well, Billy Bumpkin stories in all those earlier years were pretty much *ad hoc*. So when I set out to write down the set of stories in this book, I thought it would be good to bring a structure with plot and character development into the picture. This book is the result.

I think for a child, there is nothing more reassuring and nothing better suited to growth and the development of self-esteem than the role of great parents. Betty lets Billy become Billy. She lets him roam and even take risks, but in the end she is always there for him. He is as sure of that as he is sure that the sun will rise tomorrow—which does not mean that he doesn't push the edges.

So if you find Billy has an extraordinary perception of life and a bond with nature, and if you follow his encounters and things happen that seem out of the ordinary—like if he talks to animals, and they talk back—that's okay. That's *romance* storytelling. And *romance* makes for great stories.

What is the intended purpose of these stories? What audience are they written for?

It is intended that these stories be read to children who are in a pre-reading stage. It is intended that they be read along with children who are in their early reading stages. And then it is intended—especially with the last three episodes—that a child can pick up this book and revisit these stories on their own.

My naïve sense, then, is that a kid is much more likely to learn to read if there is something to read that is:

- Accessible, and

- If he or she *wants* to read it.

Reading is sometimes considered a *thing that only nerds do,* for god only knows what all psychosocial reasons. But if Billy Bumpkin stories have some fantastical elements and some danger and some winning and in the end a lot of security, my thought is that they might make fun reading for young readers under, say, the age of sixteen.

In overall scope, the book has to raise some questions, and then direct itself to answers. It has to challenge the reader in new ways. And it has to make us finally arrive at more fundamental questions about ourselves and why we are here.

I hope that many parents and young readers find the book enjoyable.

David J. Murphy, February, 2013

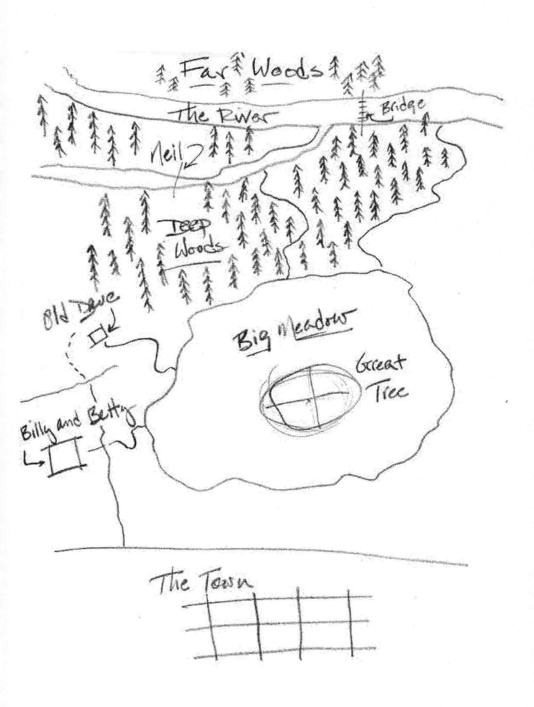

THE STORY OF
BILLY BUMPKIN AND THE COOKIES
Billy Age 7

Once upon a time, there was a brave little boy named Billy Bumpkin, whom everyone would have loved. He lived in the country, as the older country used to be. Small villages there were connected by isolated cottages that sat in clean meadows, and little boys could walk the country lanes and pathways. Young fellows his age were taught not to trust strangers and – above all – to stay out of the deep woods. But, then again, Billy was a brave little boy and, as little boys will do, he perhaps too often sought his excitement in adventure.

The creatures in the streams that ran through the meadows were his friends. He listened closely to the birds and paid attention to their song. The wind would tell him things, and he would crawl up to rest in the crook of a tree branch and feel at home.

But on occasion, usually if he had wandered farther than he should have and too close to the forest, he might encounter people or animals who were not happy. Some were children who were simply sad and lonely. Others were animals who were angry or afraid, and they could be frightening.

Billy had come to understand that he had an unusual gift for talking with people or animals who were sad and lonely or frightening. Where this gift came from, he was not sure, but he had a pretty certain guess. His mom was named Betty

Bumpkin and she was simply the most wonderful person he had ever known. Billy loved his mom with an abiding and deep love that was certain to last forever. Whenever he drew her a picture, she would admire his skill. Whenever he sang her a song, she would tell him, "What a beautiful voice you have!" And especially whenever he had a question, or faced an inexplicable fear, she would explain the mysteries of life to him and settle his discomfort, and show him once again how much she knew about the mysteries of life and the secrets of the heart. Billy suspected that his mom was the source of his gift.

And when Billy in his adventures encountered a problem too big for him to handle – like a person who was too sad and lonely or an animal who was too frightening – and when even his mom Betty was stumped, she had a special resource upon which to draw. Because, you see, Betty Bumpkin could make her own, special "Magic Be-Nice" cookies. Her "Magic Be-Nice" cookies were so good and so special and made with so much love and care that they could help lift people and even animals over their problems. Sad children could find joy by eating one. Lonely people could find company over a plate of them. Frightened, fierce animals could see their world in a cheerier light at the mere aroma of her cookies.

It wasn't just that Billy liked his mom's cookies. Everybody liked them! The gift for Billy was seeing that his mom had worked so carefully and so lovingly to develop her recipe for helping people in difficulty. As Billy grew, he decided for himself, "Now *that's* a wonderful thing to learn how to do!"

EPISODE 1
BILLY BUMPKIN GOES FOR A WALK
Billy Age 7

Billy sat in his mom's kitchen. The smell of baking bread filled the kitchen, because she was baking two loaves in the oven. Now she was preparing to bake her special Magic Be-Nice cookies.

Betty Bumpkin mixed flour and butter and sugar and eggs. Then she made a flat sheet of dough, and now she was working it with her hands. She pushed on it with the heel of her hand, and then she folded the flat sheet of dough. Then she stretched it out again and pushed on it with the heel of her hand.

She had a line of small bottles in front of her that held things Billy had watched her mix into the cookies before. Above her on a shelf were more little bottles. Lots of little bottles! She would carefully inspect the dough and then—almost without looking—reach for a bottle and sprinkle something more into the dough. Then she would stop and think and then reach for another bottle and sprinkle something more into the dough.

"Mom," said Billy.

Betty looked over at him and smiled her radiant smile. "Yes, Billy?"

"How do you know how to make bread?"

"I learned how from my own mom, honey," she said.

That would mean Grandma Betty. She had died a while ago. *Passed away*, everybody called it, and it had made everybody sad and made his mom cry for two whole days.

"How did Grandma Betty learn how to bake bread?"

"She learned from her mom, and her mom learned from her own mom," said Betty. She was working the cookie dough again. "Baking bread is just something families do. It's been that way forever. It's like picking apples and milking cows. You can read about it in special books like the Bible."

Billy thought about what she had said. There just seemed to be so much to learn about life.

Billy slipped off his stool and walked to the front door and out into the beautiful day. Just down from the front of the house were a narrow road and a small tree, and where the sunlight fell it made shade. Billy walked out to the shade in the road.

I can't wait to learn more about all this, he thought.

Just down the road to his left, he saw a rabbit. A pretty big rabbit. He turned and walked down to see it from closer up. The rabbit had mostly gray fur, with white on his chest and tummy and a little bit of brown at the bottom of each ear. The rabbit watched Billy come closer. Then, without much effort, he turned and hopped a little way down the road. There he turned and looked back at Billy. Then he hopped a little more. He kept this up.

Hippity-hop, Hippity-hop. Turn and look.

Hippity-hop, Hippity-hop. Turn and look.

Hippity-hop, Hippity-hop.

Billy followed Mr. Rabbit down the road. The rabbit turned down a path, and Billy followed him some more. This was fun. After a while, Billy lost track of time.

Finally the rabbit stopped. He sat up on his long, skinny hind legs and sniffed the air and looked at Billy. Billy looked around. He looked around and he sniffed the air, too, just like the rabbit, but he didn't smell anything special.

But he realized for sure that he was lost.

He looked around in every direction, but he didn't see anything special or anything he recognized. Then his eye caught a small house up a shallow hillside. The front door was opening and an older man stepped out. The man looked across at him.

The man started walking toward him. "Stop there, little boy!" he called out.

Billy looked down the path to the big rabbit, who still sat there, just watching. Then Billy looked back at the man, who was quickly getting closer.

Billy turned the other way on the path from the rabbit, and he ran. He ran as fast as his young legs could run. "Stop!" he heard the man yell. "Stop, boy!"

Billy ran blindly up the path, headlong with fear, back the way he had come. He turned down another path, and then he came to one that he thought maybe he recognized. Behind him—quite a way off—he heard the man calling out.

"Where are you, little boy? Where are you?"

Billy turned up the path he thought he recognized, and he ran again. He ran until he was too tired to run. Then he stopped and bent over with his hands on his knees, dragging in great breaths of air. Now what to do? He looked down at a small creek and across a small field. There he recognized the little road that ran by his mom's house.

He walked quickly down to the creek. As he hopped across, a big old frog croaked at him.

"Ribbit!"

Billy walked up the field to the little road and there, walking toward him, was his mom with a big worried smile on her face. He ran up to her and threw his arms around her waist, and she hugged him. He hugged her back and drew in strength and safety from her like a young root draws in water. "Oh, Mom!" he said.

"My, my, my!" she said. "Where did *you* get off to?"

So when he caught his breath, he told her about the beautiful day and the big old rabbit and the fun chase and the paths and then how he realized he was lost and how that scared him. Then he told her about the older man who had chased him and leaping across the creek, where the frog croaked at him.

Betty looked at him and listened as he talked. Then she said, "Well, that older man was a friend that we call Old Dave. He called me and said he had a lost-looking young boy out in front of his house, and he thought it might be you. So we need to go meet him and say thanks." And with that, she took Billy's hand. They walked back down the lane and then took some twisty paths through the woods. At one point, Billy thought he spotted the old rabbit, sitting on his long, skinny feet and peering at them with black eyes and sniffling with his nose.

They came to the older man's home. He stood up from his chair on the front porch and waved and walked down to meet them. "Well, young fellow," he said, "I'm sure glad you found your mom," and he smiled down at Billy. "Come on inside."

Betty had brought half a loaf of bread and a few cookies for Old Dave, so they sat down at a square table and split a big cookie. Old Dave brought Billy a small glass of milk that tasted really good.

After a few minutes, Old Dave looked at Billy. "You just want to be sure that you when go wandering, boy, you always make certain of the way home. 'Specially when you have a mom at home as special as your mom," and he smiled at Billy again.

After that, Billy and Betty walked back home. That evening Betty served some rice with a stew made of celery and carrots and small red potatoes and a little bit of beef. Billy took a shower, and she walked him to bed and began to read him a story. Before she got to the bottom of the first page, he fell sound asleep and slept the whole night through.

EPISODE 2

BILLY BUMPKIN AND BIG MIKE AND THE BIG YELLOW TRUCK

Billy Age 7

Billy's mom came into his room one morning. She shook him gently by the shoulder to wake him up. The sunlight of a brilliant new day flooded into his room. He could see dust floating in the air in the warm, golden beams. Betty Bumpkin sat down on the bed next to Billy.

"We have a wonderful little trip to take today. We're going to walk into town and meet a man with a big, wonderful yellow truck!" she said.

"Okay, mom! That sounds great," said Billy. Like all little boys, Billy loved big trucks. So he hopped out of bed and went to the bathroom and then pulled off his pajamas. He put on the T-shirt and the jeans that Betty had laid out for him. Then he pulled on his socks and then his sneakers, taking time to get them tied just right.

Betty had breakfast waiting for him: a banana and a hard-boiled egg. When he was finished, she went into the living room for her purse. She hung the purse on a hook by the door. Then she went back to the kitchen and reemerged carrying a school-lunch-size paper bag. "Here we go!" she said.

As they walked down their little road toward town, they talked about the butterflies that they saw, and she told Billy the names of the flowers that grew in glorious profusion alongside the road. Billy was always amazed that his mom knew so much about just about everything.

Betty held Billy's hand. They walked all the way to town and then into the heart of downtown. They came to a big city block that had been cleared. Stacks of building materials lay inside a high chain-link fence, and there were trucks and machines all around. One of the trucks was a big yellow truck.

They were met at a gate in the fence by a big man with short blond hair and a bright, warm smile. He had blue eyes. He was wearing jeans and boots and a button-up denim shirt. He wore a deep-red kerchief around his neck with a pattern of little designs on it in alternating black and white. "Billy," said his mom, "this is Big Mike. He's a friend of ours."

"Hi, Billy," said Big Mike.

"Hi, Big Mike," said Billy. He stuck out his small hand, and Big Mike stuck out his huge hand, and they shook hands. Big Mike led Betty and Billy over to a stack of wide planks, and they sat on them like a bench. Betty opened the bag she had brought. She pulled out a Magic Be-Nice cookie for Big Mike and then one for Billy and then one for herself. They all took bites of their cookies.

After a few minutes, Billy got up and wandered out toward the middle of the big empty plot of dirt. There were little stakes in the ground and red ribbon tied to them that ran from one stake to another. Billy stepped over the ribbon.

Suddenly he heard Big Mike say, "Be careful there, Billy!" It startled him, and Billy glanced around to see what Big Mike had been talking about.

Big Mike walked over to him. "You're standing in the elevator shaft," he said, and he laughed gently. Billy looked back up at him.

"When we build this building, there will be a shaft here that will go from well below the ground all the way up to the roof. See the outer rows of the stakes and the ribbon? That shows where the outside walls will be."

Billy looked around. All the nearby buildings were four or five stories tall, so he guessed that's what this one would be too.

"And these other stakes and ribbons?" said Big Mike. "This is where the big support beams will go and where usually the inside walls would be. Follow me. Let me show you something." They walked over to a big stack of heavy metal beams. "These will be the support beams. They will hold the building up. Other beams will lie across them and support the floors as they go up. Here, try and pick one up."

Billy put his hands on a beam, and he could not budge it an inch. Big Mike smiled. "I know. They're really, really heavy."

Billy walked back to the spot where the elevator shaft would one day be and he looked up. He realized he could just about see the square shaft rising up above him toward the sky. Then he looked down and realized that the ground would be gone, and he would be hanging over a deep, empty shaft. He looked around again, and in his mind's eye he could see walls and pipes and wires.

"Where's the elevator car?" he asked Big Mike.

"Oh, it'll come one day. It's a block-shaped car that gets pulled up and let down by steel cables, and it runs on little wheels that run in channels in the shaftwall corners. Don't worry," he smiled. "It's very safe. It won't fall on you!" Still, Billy moved a few steps over to his right.

Just to be out of where the shaft was going to be.

He looked back up and saw the elevator shaft again, hollow and huge and reaching high, high up into the sky. As he watched, the elevator shaft changed into a giant rocket, with a space ship on top. It was white with a flag painted on it, and had fins on the sides. Before his eyes, the rocket changed into a tall tree reaching almost to the sky itself, with branches that reached out far over the city. He looked around and saw, instead of the drab and weepy storefronts of the small town, a bustling city with tall church spires and shiny, multi-story buildings with people bustling in and out and waving at each other and calling out and smiling.

Suddenly there was a loud, violent thunderclap that shook his body like his Mom waking him in the morning. And it was real. It was not in his imagination. In an instant Big Mike was at his side. "C'mon, Billy," he said. "There must be a storm up the valley. Sometimes lightning and thunder can happen away from the storm center." He walked Billy back over to his Mom.

Billy saw Big Mike look around at the sky. "Funny," Big Mike said to Betty, "not a cloud up there. That thunder came out of nowhere!"

Betty had been watching from beside the stack of planks where they had eaten their cookies. She looked at Billy, and she had a funny, curious smile on her face. Big Mike said, "C'mon. I've got a few minutes. I'll give you two a lift to start you on your way home."

They walked outside the fence and came to the big yellow truck.

"Is this yours?" Billy asked.

"Yup," said Big Mike, and he moved to open the passenger door for Betty.

"What makes it run?" asked Billy.

Big Mike paused and looked down at him. "You really like to learn things, don't you?"

"I want to learn a lot about everything," said Billy.

"Oh, really!" said Big Mike. "So what are some of the things you've already learned?"

"Well, I've learned there's winter and summer, and they're very different from each other."

"Yes."

"And I've learned there's the town and the country, and they're different from each other too."

"Yes."

"And I've learned about plants and animals, and the bigger animals and the smaller animals and how they have to live together. And I've learned about different kinds of birds and even some about snakes, but I don't know much about fish."

"Wow."

"And I don't know how to cook. And I don't know how my mom knows so much about everything."

Big Mike looked at Betty and smiled.

At the truck, Big Mike opened the driver's door and reached beneath the dash and pulled something, and Billy heard a pop in the front of the truck. Big Mike lifted the hood, which was hinged at the front, and propped it open with a rod. Then he picked Billy up like he weighed nothing at all and set him on his knees on the top of the front fender. Billy looked down on a welter of covers and wires and little pipes, all covering a massive piece of metal.

"That's the engine," said Big Mike. "It burns fuel that comes in through this little line here, sort of like your mom burns wood in her fireplace. That creates turns in the engine that connect to gears and stuff that run back to the back end of the truck and turn the wheels. It's a little more complicated than that, but that's what actually makes the truck run."

Mike lifted Billy again and this time carried him around to the passenger door. Betty climbed into the passenger seat, and Mike lifted Billy up into her lap.

"Here you go," he said. "You'll see pretty good from up here." Then Mike walked around to the driver's side and climbed behind the wheel. He turned the key, and the truck started with a deep rumble. He looked at Billy and then pointed to a lanyard that hung down from the ceiling of the cab.

"See that?" he said.

"Yes."

"Give it a pull." Billy pulled the lanyard, and a horn made a loud burst of sound, "Toot!"

Mike said, "Here, do it like this." He gave the lanyard two short pulls and then a long one.

"Toot! Toot! TOOOOOT!"

Billy did the same thing.

"Toot! Toot! TOOOOOT!"

"Everybody knows that means Big Mike's rollin'!" said Mike with a big grin, and they drove off through the town.

Billy and Betty did not have a car or a truck. Billy had certainly never ridden in any vehicle this massive. Sitting in his mom's lap, it felt funny to look down on the tops of people who were walking on the sidewalk.

The big truck jounced as it drove along. "It rides smoother when it's full of dirt," said Mike.

Billy watched as the scenery went past at this unusual height. He thought about what he had seen when he was looking up, back at the construction site. When they got near Betty's home, Mike pulled over and let them out. "That little road in front of your house is too small for this great big truck," he told Billy. "Thanks, young man. That was a wonderful visit! Look, here's a little something to remember today by…" Big Mike reached up and untied the kerchief that he wore. He leaned over and circled it loosely around Billy's neck and tied a soft knot. He said, "There! Now you look like a guy who rides around with Big Mike in the Big Yellow Truck!" Billy and Betty laughed, and then they got out of the cab. Big Mike turned around and waved out the window, and headed back toward town.

Billy and Betty walked the short way home holding hands. They spent some time in the afternoon talking about what a great visit they had had with Big Mike. Then they worked with numbers for a little while, and then Betty gave Billy some time to read. She made a small meatloaf for dinner with mashed potatoes and gravy, along with broccoli. Billy liked broccoli.

After dinner Billy took a shower and then he read a little more. He came back to the kitchen and calmly told his mother what he had seen when he was looking up at the elevator shaft. "It was like I could see stuff before it was even there," he said.

Betty looked at him with a huge, warm smile on her face, and her eyes suddenly glistened. "You are so like your father, Billy. He could see things that other people couldn't see, just like you."

"My father? Are you going to talk about my father?"

Betty was quiet as she just looked at him. Storms crossed over her face. He had never seen her be quite like this before. "Ah! There's a lot to talk about there, honey, but it's late. When we talk about all that, it will take time, and you should probably be a little older. He was a wonderful man, Billy, just like you will be someday."

Then his mom led him to his bed, and they sang a song about birds in a field of green, with bright, sunlit daffodils and a trout that swam by in a stream and sang to a little boy.

Betty looked at Billy with a straight face and held up her right hand and said, "I swear this is true!", though Billy had long suspected she was just storytelling.

Then she pulled his covers up and told him she loved him. She turned out his light, and as she walked out of his room, she turned and said, "Sleep tight, Billy. I'll be right here if you need me."

Billy lay on his side under his covers, and there he felt safe from all the devils who threaten to snatch little boys' souls in the deep, deep dark. And then he closed his eyes and slept soundly, all through the long and holy night.

EPISODE 3

BILLY AND THE BIG GRAY RABBIT

Billy Age 8

Billy sat in the nook of a tree branch and watched life in the big meadow. Here are some of the things he saw and heard.

He heard the gentle rustle of the wind in the leaves of the great tree where he sat. He heard the birds chirping all of their different chirps, from wrens to cardinals to finches to rattling woodpeckers. He heard the *chick-chucking* of the squirrels and the rustle of the field mice and the occasional *yips* of the newborn foxes, off near the tree line.

Normally in the morning, Billy and his mom, Betty Bumpkin, would walk up to the small store and purchase any food they needed for the day. They would buy milk and eggs and cheese, and maybe a small piece of beef or lamb or pork—always small, because it was just for the two of them. They would walk up the narrow lane outside their house holding hands and talking. They would buy what they needed. And then they would walk back home holding hands.

Then one day his mom, who knew more about the secrets of life and the mysteries of the heart than anyone else on earth, said to Billy, "If you'd like, go spend a little time in the meadow. It might be good for you. Then come home—I'll have lunch

17

for us, and then you can read to me." And that became their new habit.

Billy felt, of course, like a new little man. He felt like he had grown up a bit. He came to love sitting in a crook of the tree—in the great tree in the middle of the big meadow, the tree with its decades of branches and its cornucopia of fruits and nuts.

Today had been another special day. He had walked up to the meadow, breathing in its special joy there in the sun-drenched glory of the morning. He had climbed into the tree and spent his hour there. Then he had started his walk home to be with his mom.

Only on this particular morning something had been different. Because, on this morning, he had been able to listen to and understand what all the wind had meant, and he understood all of what the animals were saying.

Billy did not tell his mom right away that he was listening to the birds and the animals and that he could understand them. For several weeks, he found it hard to believe himself. So he kept up his habit of going to the meadow and sitting in the tree.

And listening.

He found that, day by day, he was more and more certain that he understood what he was hearing. He understood the animals better and better. So one day he told his mom.

"Mom, can I tell you something?"

"Sure, honey," said Betty. "What's on your mind?"

"Well, when I sit in the big tree—up there in the meadow?—I can listen to the birds and the animals, and I understand what they're saying to each other. Is that okay?"

His mom gave him a funny look, but not a look without a smile behind it. "Well, what do you hear them talking about?"

"Oh, they talk about their babies and they talk about food, mostly. Then they talk about what time of day it is, what time of year, whether the moon is full or not, when it's gonna get cold, that sort of thing. And they warn each other of any predators that might be around."

Betty looked at him and then took both of his hands in hers. "Well, I guess we should all be good listeners, honey. Do you feel like it's okay?"

Billy thought about that for a moment. "I worry that I'm kind of eavesdropping, maybe. But I've just been so amazed at what I could hear and understand...!"

"Well," said Betty, "here's my rule. Whatever you can do with special talents, as long as you use those special talents to help others, then that's a good thing for everybody." And she smiled her radiant smile at him, and he drew strength from her smile and from holding her hands.

So Billy kept going to the meadow, and he kept listening to the birds and to the wind and to the animals.

One early afternoon, just after lunch, Billy heard a thumping noise outside the front door. At first he ignored it, but the noise continued.

Thump! Thump! Pause. *Thump! Thump!* Pause. *Thump! Thump!*

So he went to the front of the house and opened the door. There at the stoop was the big gray rabbit, the one he had followed down the lane over a year before. The rabbit looked at Billy, and Billy looked back.

"Follow me," said the rabbit, and he turned and started to slowly hop toward the meadow.

Lippety, lippety.

He stopped and looked back at Billy, who had not moved from the stoop.

"They need you," said the rabbit.

He hopped slowly toward the meadow again.

Lippety, lippety.

"Who needs me?" Billy called out.

The rabbit looked back. "The birds," he said.

Imagine being Billy, standing there alone on that stoop, with a rabbit talking to him!

The rabbit stared at him. "They know you listen," he said. "They need you. They trust you. Come along now."

Billy thought for a moment. Then he turned to the front door and called inside.

"Mom! I'm going up to the meadow for a few minutes, okay?"

Betty came into the front room, wiping her hands with a cotton dish towel.

"Is everything all right?" she said.

"Yes, ma'am. I'm just going to follow the old gray rabbit up there."

Betty listened calmly and paused and then said, "Okay, honey. You just be careful, and call if you need me."

Billy ran after the rabbit, who now picked up speed himself. "Nest fell from the tree," he said over his shoulder.

Lippety, lippety. Faster! Faster!

"Not much time!"

Billy followed the rabbit. The path wound around trees, new and old, and then under the branches of the dogwood grove, where the trees had shed their white blossoms a month or so before.

Their blossoms look like crosses, the dogwoods do, Billy had told his mom one night after she had read him a Bible story.

Up, up the hillside they ran, until they reached the edge of the meadow.

The rabbit led Billy to a maple tree a long way off to the west of where his path entered the meadow. He would never have had reason to wander off in that direction, but the old rabbit moved to the tree like a dart. The branches were filled with finches, talking worriedly among themselves.

On the ground was a nest. It had three blue eggs in it. None of the eggs was broken.

"Eggs, the eggs are getting cold," said the rabbit. "We have to get the nest back up into the tree. Or the eggs will die, or a snake will get them."

Billy looked at the tree. The lowest branches were stout, but they sprang from the bole over eight feet above the ground.

"But I can't touch the nest," he said to the rabbit.

"Do what you can to help," the rabbit said. "These are surely the last eggs of the season. You can see and you can hear—the finches are very worried."

Billy looked back at the tree. He thought and he thought. Then he said to the rabbit, "I think I have an idea."

Then he turned and ran across the meadow to the head of the path. Then he flew as fast as a bird himself, down the path toward the house and his mom.

He arrived back at the tree a short time later with his mom. She had brought a clean cotton dish towel, some clear plastic wrap, and a pair of brand-new rubber gloves. Billy told the rabbit to warn the other animals that there were human things he and his mom had to do, and it might be disturbing. Without protest, the birds and squirrels and field mice began pulling back into the silent forest, creating a space for Billy and his mom to work.

Then Old Dave appeared. He carried a folding stepladder on his shoulder.

When Billy had reached the house and Betty, he had blurted out a story to her about talking to the animals and a bird's nest.

"They need our help," he kept insisting.

She got him to take a few deep breaths and then had him tell the story over again, calmly and in detail. Then she had thought through the problem, which he knew she would do. And then together they had formulated a plan. And she had put in a phone call to Old Dave. Billy had listened.

"Just go with me on this," she had said to Old Dave.

Billy put on the rubber gloves, because he and Betty were concerned that the animals would trust no one but Billy. Then he laid the cotton dish towel on the ground and then he pushed on it and turned it over and pushed on it again, trying to get the human smell out and the smell of the earth into the weave. Then he stretched out a piece of the plastic wrap. He looked off into the trees and listened.

"No, he's doing it right," he thought he heard a squirrel say. "You can't trust a human," he thought he heard an old crow whisper. "He's the only one we *can* trust. He *listens* to us…!" said the female robin.

Billy carefully lifted the bird's nest by two edges and moved it swiftly to the plastic wrap. Old Dave set up the ladder beside the trunk of the tree. Then he asked Billy to tell him once again where he was headed when he got up into the tree.

"Where we talked about," said Billy. He pointed to a branch with a fork about fifteen feet up into the tree. "Right there," he said.

"I'll be right down here, young fellow," said Old Dave. "But best you don't fall," and he smiled.

Billy put his hand under the dish towel, which was under the nest with its three eggs. He took careful steps up the ladder. When he reached the first strong branch, he braced himself with a hand on the next branch above and looked down at the rabbit.

"They're thanking you," he heard the rabbit say. Betty and Old Dave seemed not to hear a thing.

Using his elbows, his one free hand, and his feet and knees, Billy climbed up into the tree, higher and higher. He reached a branch below the fork he had targeted. He inched out onto the branch, still balancing the three eggs in their nest.

Very carefully, he rested the nest into the "Y" of the fork, and then withdrew the dish towel and the plastic wrap from beneath the nest. He looked down at Old Dave and Betty. Old Dave smiled and gave him a thumbs-up, and then put his two palms out as if to say, "Careful now on the way down."

Billy suddenly felt sort of clammy, so he stopped looking down. He eased back along the branch to the bole of the tree, and then very cautiously he felt his way down with his feet. He didn't want to look down again.

Finally he felt his right foot touch the top of the ladder, and then the topmost step. Then he felt a hand gently grabbing him by the belt at the small of his back, and he knew that he was in the strong grip of Old Dave. Secure in the man's grasp, he descended the ladder and finally stood safely on the ground beside his mom.

He heard the gray rabbit say, "Now you should go. All of this scares the animals of the meadow. They don't trust anyone but you. And they thank you, each and every one."

That night Billy took a shower and then his mom followed him to his room and they read *In the Night Kitchen* because it was so much fun, and then she kissed him and then she turned out the light.

And in the night, it may be that Betty Bumpkin looked in on him. And it may be that she wondered how she happened to have such a special and blessed little boy. And probably then she said a brief but genuine prayer of humble gratitude and thanksgiving.

But Billy would not have known, because he was a very tired young fellow. And he slept. And he slept.

EPISODE 4

Billy Bumpkin and Carl the Rat
Billy Age 9

Not far from Billy Bumpkin's house, where he lived with his mom, Betty Bumpkin, there was a great tree, with decades of branches and millions of leaves and nuts and acorns and fruit. The tree had soft earth around it. In that soft earth lived a rat named Carl. Billy knew who Carl was. The field mice had told Billy about him.

Carl was a fat, slow rat with wretched brown fur. His snout was long and ugly, and he had twitchy whiskers that stuck out behind his runny nose. He had sharp teeth, and even for a rat his breath was dreadful.

All around the tree were fields and meadows with tall grass and happy wildflowers. Sometimes deer would show up to eat the grasses, and for dessert they would munch on the fruits and nuts. Those grasses were where the field mice lived. Billy liked to visit the fields. He talked and played with the field mice. He would go to the meadow on warm afternoons with seeds in his hand, like fennel and poppy. The mice would sit up on their bottoms with their tiny front feet in the air and welcome Billy in quick jabbers. They would say, "Jabber! Jabber! Jabber!" and Billy would sprinkle some fennel or poppy seeds for them. He came to know the mommy mice and also their baby mice. Then he would collect a bouquet of wildflowers and take them home as a surprise for his mom, and then she would make the two of them a delicious and healthy dinner.

He also learned from the mice more about Carl, the local rat. The mice told him, first, because sometimes they would jabber and sniff the seed Billy had brought, but then look around like they were scared. Then they would just scurry off.

Sometimes Billy would climb up into the decades of branches on the big old tree and watch the animals play in the meadow. And then one day, he saw Carl the Rat frightening the field mice away. Billy, who was a brave little boy, let himself down quietly from the bottom branches and came up behind Carl.

"Why did you scare the mice away? You didn't even eat the fennel and poppy seed."

"I don't want to eat those stupid seeds," said Carl. "Those are for little mousy mice, and I'm no mousy mouse."

"But then, why do you scare the mice away?" said Billy.

"Hey, if I don't want to like the seed, then I don't want them to like it either. And besides, I'm bigger, so why shouldn't I scare them away…You better leave me alone, or I'll scare you away, too."

"Then what do you eat?" asked Billy. "Your fur looks wretched, and your nose is runny, and even from here I can smell your bad breath. Yuck!"

"Oh, there's a dead skunk in an old mud-pile over there behind the tree. I stick my nose in the mud and dig around and eat what I find. What do you care?"

Billy did not pick a bouquet of flowers that day. Instead, he went home to talk to his mom about the rat and his terrible behavior. You see, Billy understood that nobody knew better than Betty Bumpkin about good and bad behavior, or more about the mysteries of the heart.

The next day, Billy set out once again for the meadow. In his pocket, he had one of Betty's uncanny Magic-Be-Nice cookies. The night before, Betty had made the suggestion after Billy told her about Carl.

"Why don't you take Carl a Magic-Be-Nice cookie tomorrow?"

"Can a Magic-Be-Nice cookie be good for a nasty rat?" Billy asked.

"I really don't know, sweetie, but they seem to really be good for nasty people…Why not give it a try?"

When Billy got to the meadow, he sprinkled around some fennel seeds and some poppy seed. Today he also had some celery seeds. The field mice appeared out of the grass and sat up on their bottoms. "Jabber! Jabber! Jabber!" they said.

But then suddenly they all looked around, and then they all scurried back into the tall grass. Carl the Rat strode boldly up to Billy. "I told you I don't want the mice to like your stupid little seeds."

Billy said, "Are you going to eat the seeds?"

"No. I told you that. I don't want to like the seeds."

"Well, then," Billy said, "I brought something else for you." And he took out the Magic-Be-Nice cookie and crumbled off a piece and put it on the ground in front of Carl.

Carl looked at the piece of cookie, which had Betty's colorful sparkles and raisins and chocolate drops and other magic ingredients.

Carl sniffed at the piece of cookie with his ugly snout and his runny nose. Then with his stiff whiskers, he brushed away the piece of cookie. "Ugh!" he said. "Who would eat a thing like that?" And then he sauntered off back toward the great tree.

Billy walked home and told Betty about Carl. "I'm sorry, sweetie. Carl sounds like he is a really, *really* not nice rat." Then she got a thoughtful, faraway look in her eyes. She put her finger up to her pursed lips, then she slowly walked around her kitchen until finally she had made an entire circle. She stopped and leaned her head down toward Billy.

"Maybe Carl didn't like the way the cookie *looked*. Maybe that was his excuse for not even giving it a taste."

"What?"

Betty turned back into her kitchen, saying over her shoulder that Billy could stay or he could go read a book. "I have work to do!" she said.

The next morning Billy headed off to the meadow again. Once again he brought fennel seed and poppy seed and celery seed. The field mice said, "Jabber! Jabber!" and came out of the tall grass and began to eat. But then they all began to look around, and shortly they scurried away, back into the grass. Billy saw Carl stick his ugly snout into the little clearing. Carl parted the grass and lumbered into the clearing. Before Carl could speak, Billy said, "Okay, I guess you just don't want to be nice. Your choice. But, I brought some other, special seeds just for you." And with that he spread different-shaped seeds on the ground. They were about the size of small pieces of popcorn, and they were small and cinnamon-colored and dimpled.

Without a word, Billy spun on his heel and walked off toward the great tree. He climbed up into its decades of branches and its canopy of breeze-filled leaves and found a comfortable nook in the dappling sunlight. He thought he might keep an eye on the meadow and see what deer or foxes decided to drop by and visit. He reached into his pocket and brought out in his hand four of the special seeds he had brought for Carl, and he popped them into his mouth. *Mmmm!* he thought. *Delicious!* Because, you see, the night before Betty had gone to work, and she had made super-special, Magic-Be-Nice *cookie drops*—just for Carl. She left off the colorful sparkles, and she left out the chocolate drops. Then she made the cookie dough with every imaginable magic ingredient that she had ever thought to add.

In each cookie drop, she included one, plump, lusty raisin, for purposes of healthy nutrition. Then she had baked the drops for Carl.

After a while, Billy climbed down out of the branches and walked back to the clearing. All of the cookie drops were gone. The field mice were nibbling up the last of the seeds he had left before. They sat up on their bottoms with their tiny front feet in the air.

"Jabber! Jabber! Jabber!" they said. Billy had a little celery seed left, so he spread that for them. They scampered from here to there and all around, filling their little cheeks.

Billy decided to head for home. At the edge of the meadow, he was confronted by Carl. "I'm leaving," said Carl.

"Where are going?" Billy said.

Carl's lips drew back over his sharp, ugly teeth into a snarl. His eyes blazed. "To some other meadow, that's where!" he said. "You're trying to change me, and I don't want to change. I'm okay the way I am!"

"I can't change you, Carl," said Billy. "My mom tells me that we are the only ones who can make ourselves choose to be nice or happy. Or both. Anyway, when you leave I think I will miss you. But good luck." And with that, Billy walked home.

After that, when Billy visited the meadow, there was no Carl to be seen. The field mice ate all their fennel seed and poppy seed in peace. And then, one morning, who should show up but Carl, waiting for Billy at the edge of the meadow.

"I'm tired of not being nice," said Carl.

Billy said nothing.

"It takes a lot of work to be mean and not nice all the time."

Billy just listened, and said nothing.

"In the other meadow, I was scared by a snake who had long fangs and hissed at me. I got chased around by a raccoon who was even meaner than me. And then there was this buzzard with an ugly beak and long talons on his feet who kept watching me with an evil eye."

Billy said nothing at first. And then he said, "C'mon" and walked off toward the clearing. He could hear Carl tagging along behind him. At the clearing, Carl put his tummy down on the ground at the edge. "I have this for you," said Billy, and he laid some Magic-Be-Nice cookie drops on the ground in front of Carl.

Billy turned to look into the clearing. It was full around the edges with field mice. The field mice looked up at Billy.

And then they looked over at Carl.

Carl ate the cookie drops.

The mice looked back up at Billy. And then they looked back over one more time at Carl. And then they sat up on their bottoms and waved their little front feet in the air.

"Jabber! Jabber! Jabber!" said the field mice.

"Welcome home," said Billy to Carl.

EPISODE 5

BILLY AND THE REALLY SMART KID
Billy Age 9

The teacher stood sternly at the front of the classroom. Her name was Mrs. Butterfield. She was slender and had hair going gray that snugged up to her head in tight, natural curls. She wore rimless glasses with lines that ran across the middle of each lens. Her jawline was cut like stone and ended in a sharp point at her chin. Her shirt was white and had pleats down the front. It was buttoned up to her neck.

"All right, children," she said. "Time for math now. And you all like a fun game, yes? So I think we should have a fun game now. Don't you?"

As one person, the kids in the class responded, "Yes, Mrs. Butterfield."

"Math contest!" said Mrs. Butterfield. She had the children's attention. "On the boys' side…" She looked around the class.

"Billy Bumpkin." Billy heard his name with mixed emotions.

"On the girls' side…" She looked around the room again. "Ann Roberts!" All of the girls clapped. If you knew the kids in Billy's class, you would know that there were normal kids, but then there were smart kids, too.

Ann Roberts was a really smart kid, the smartest girl in the class.

Mrs. Butterfield arched her eyebrows in a conspiratorial smile. "The…" she paused. "The twelve-times table!"

And all the kids gasped and laughed and shouted.

Billy looked over at Ann. She was looking at him. With a grin, she slid out from behind her desk. She wore black-and-white shoes and thin white socks turned down neatly at the top. She wore a plaid jumper and a white shirt. Her hair was long and parted on the right side, held back by a barrette with a rose on it.

"Billy?" said Mrs. Butterfield. Billy shifted his eyes quickly left and then right. There was only one thing he could do, so he stood up.

Billy felt all the boys in the class looking at him. He was afraid he might not win the contest.

"Ann, you and Billy start when I say, 'go!'" Mrs. Butterfield raised her right hand at a sharp angle, then dropped it straight down like a butcher knife and said, "Go!"

"Twelve times one is twelve," Billy and Ann both said.

"Twelve times two is twenty-four. Twelve times three is thirty-six."

Billy had been in a spelling bee two weeks before. He and Betty Ann Winedelts had been the last two kids standing at the front of the room. Billy had misspelled "carriage." Betty Ann got the word "neighborhood" and spelled it right and won for the girls' side. Thinking about this, Billy stumbled on twelve times four, so Ann got a little ahead of him.

Not everyone can be perfect every time, he thought. Then Ann stumbled on twelve times nine.

Billy didn't think that Mrs. Butterfield really liked him. First of all, he was a boy, and Mrs. Butterfield liked the girls better, or at least that's what the boys all told each other. He sat by the windows because the class always sat in alphabetical order, and his last name started with a B. In second grade, he had noticed that the sun did not go up as many panes in the window in mid-winter as it did in September and in May, and he wondered why, so he kept watching. In third grade, Mrs. Butterfield got after him for staring out the window and not paying attention.

Then just yesterday the class had been in the library, and Billy had wandered into the fifth-grade section. He found a book about Daniel Boone and pulled it off the shelf and began to flip through the pages. Mrs. Butterfield found him and told him he was in the wrong section and to come back with her. At the end of the day, she gave him a note and said, "Take this home to your mother and have her sign it and bring it back tomorrow."

So Billy had taken the note home and told his mom, Betty Bumpkin, that she was supposed to read it. As she did, a smile crept slowly over her face. She pulled a pen out of a drawer and wrote something back on the note and said, "I love you so much, Billy, just the way you are. Take this note back to Mrs. Butterfield tomorrow." And so he had, along with his lunch that she had made and one of her special Magic-Be-Nice cookies.

"Twelve times eleven is a hundred thirty-two," he said, and as fast as he could, he added, "Twelve times twelve is a hundred forty-four," because Ann was catching up. But Billy finished first. All the boys cheered and started swapping high fives.

At the end of the day, Billy waited outside of school for Ann to come out. Her hair was still parted perfectly on the right and the barrette with the rose was still in place.

"I thought you might want a snack," he said, and he offered her half of his mom's special cookie.

She looked at him and smiled and took the cookie. "Thanks," she said. "See you tomorrow."

"Yeah, see you tomorrow," said Billy.

On the way home, Billy passed through the large meadow with the great tree and stopped in a clearing in the shadow of the tree. After a moment, a large clan of field mice scurried into the clearing.

"Jabber! Jabber! Jabber!" they said.

Billy crumbled up the last half of his cookie and sprinkled it over the ground. The field mice gobbled up the crumbs and sat on their hind legs and chewed and sniffed and found more crumbs to gobble until they were all gone. Then they disappeared into the wild grass and flowers.

I like it so much better here than at school, thought Billy. He wondered if he should talk to his mom Betty about this when he got home. He decided that he would, because she knew so much about life.

EPISODE 6

BILLY AND THE BELLICOSE SQUIRRELS

Billy Age 10

Billy was walking in the deep woods in the afternoon of an early autumn day. The air was noticeably cool, and the leaves were advanced in their turning. It was in his mind that he should probably be heading for home when suddenly the forest got very quiet. Billy thought he heard a stirring off in the underbrush to his right. He looked that way but couldn't see anything. Then he heard a rustling in the branches above him. Again, he couldn't see anything.

Bu then he saw, in the path about ten feet ahead of him, a furry gray squirrel. A very *big* furry gray squirrel, as a matter of fact. The squirrel was almost a foot and a half tall when he sat back on his haunches. He had a mean scowl on his face.

"Who are *you*? And what are you doing here?" said the squirrel.

"My name is Billy Bumpkin, and all I'm doing is taking a walk in the woods," said Billy.

"Well, we're the gray squirrels, and we don't like to be disturbed in our part of the woods!" His eyes narrowed, but the scowl remained. "So why don't you just leave."

Here was something new for Billy—a hostile squirrel. "Okay," he said, "I told you my name—why don't you tell me yours?"

The squirrel drew himself up on his hind legs and said, "My name is Drk Cha, and I'm the boss in this part of the woods." He pronounced the first name almost like *Dirk*, but when he said it along with his last name, it sounded just like the chucking sort of noise that Billy heard at home out in the trees all the time. The squirrel continued to glare at Billy.

"So I think it's time for you to go, young boy. And if I were you, I wouldn't come back this way. We may not look very big to you, but let me tell you, we have some big friends in the woods, and when they want to, they can be very *un*-friendly to people like you, if you catch what I mean.

"And if we think we catch you even *thinking* about talking to the black squirrels, I'll make *sure* my big friends take care of you!"

The last thing Billy needed was to catch a bunch of trouble from a big gray squirrel, so without a word, he turned and started back toward home. He had walked quite a way when he noticed the woods go quiet around him again. He peered left and then he peered right. And then he peered up into the branches that were overhead and around him, but he could see no sign of being observed.

Only the silence spoke to him.

He came around a bend in the path, and there in front of him was another squirrel. This one was about the same height as Drk Cha, but his fur was much darker. Also different was the fur on his chest, which was, surprisingly, a pale yellow in color. This squirrel stood on his hind feet to his full height and with a forepaw leaned casually against the trunk of a tree.

"So," he said. "I heard you met Drk Cha. That squirrel's a real piece of work, isn't he? What did you think of him?"

Well, what a day for meeting odd squirrels! thought Billy. "My name is Billy Bumpkin," he said.

"I know. I heard that, too," said the dark squirrel. "So. What did you think of Drk Cha?"

"Well, I don't know what to think," said Billy. "What's up with his attitude, I guess is what I think. Because he didn't explain anything to me. And who are you? Are you one of the black squirrels that he talked about?"

The squirrel laughed a dismissive laugh. "Look at me—do I look like a black squirrel to you? Yeah, the color of my fur is a little different than his, but I like to think I'm a lot smarter and a lot nicer guy than he is. My name is Chk Yah, by the way." He pronounced *Chk* almost like "Chick," but—like Drk Cha—when he said his name, it came out sounding like the familiar sound of a squirrel out in the trees.

Billy pressed his question again. "So really. What is it that bothers him? What's going on in these woods?"

Chk Yah stepped away from the tree and brushed the palms of his forepaws to clean them. He paused and looked around.

"Look around you and tell me what you see," he said.

Billy looked around and said nothing.

"Okay, what time of the year is it?"

Again Billy said nothing.

"Hello! Getting colder? Days getting shorter? What, maybe two months and it'll snow? Look, this is the time of the year when us squirrels have to pack away food for the winter, right? I mean, let's face it, no one's gonna bring Thanksgiving dinner out to us, right? No chocolate almonds or fruitcake for us come Christmas, you think?"

Billy got it. "But what does this have to do with Drk Cha and the gray squirrels?"

Chk Yah tossed his forepaws into the air. "Kid, are you dense or what? Drk Cha wants the whole woods to forage in! Just for him and his gray squirrels!"

"But that … that wouldn't be … but what are the black squirrels supposed to live on? When winter comes?"

"Finally," said Chk Yah, "some common sense from you."

"Why won't he just share?" asked Billy.

The big black squirrel rested back on one hind leg and crossed his forepaws across his chest.

"Well, he tells us that the gray squirrels were here first and it was their woods, and then us darker squirrels came in and had no right to do so, and so now we have no right to the forage for winter food stocks."

"Is that true?"

"Is it *true*? I don't know. We slowly came this way as a big family of squirrels. The first time I saw a gray squirrel was just that—the first time I ever saw a gray squirrel. Look, the fact is, there is plenty of winter forage for all the two groups of squirrels to share. And what I really think? I think it's a lot easier to gather winter stocks if you have the whole woods to gather from. I think it might be just a little more work to dig a little harder in a smaller space.

"I mean, I think *that's* what's really going on, but Drk Cha's not going to just come out and say that."

Billy had never been confronted by a situation like this. What was he supposed to do? Anything at all? Was he supposed to say something? Why had these two squirrels said these things to *him*? "I need to be headed home now," he simply said.

Chk Yah smiled back at him. "Yeah, I know—why am I telling you all about this anyway? Hey, look, kid, you come back out to these woods anytime you want. Love to see you, really, love to see you. That is, you may not see *us*, but we'll be happy to see *you*." He laughed at his own little joke.

"But Drk Cha told you about his mean friends, and he was serious about that. He knows a few tough snakes and raccoons, and you probably really want to stay away from him, okay? Okay, Billy. Have a nice day."

Billy walked home with turmoil in his thoughts. He took a path that led him to the big meadow where the great tree was. He thought about the field mice and Carl the Rat and wondered how it was that they could get along, but not the squirrels.

When he got home, he told his mom, Betty, about his strange encounter with the squirrels.

She said, "Just how deep did you go into the woods, honey?"

"Oh, a little ways, but not all that far."

"Okay," she said, "but you know it can be dangerous in the deep woods. I've always given you space to explore your world, but I also trust you to know to stay safe."

Billy gave his mom a big hug. "I love you, mom," he said. And as always he drew great comfort from Betty, who knew so much about how life worked.

He just didn't understand why the squirrels had to have this big disagreement.

By the next morning, Billy had an idea. He took some of the cookie drops that his mom made for Carl and walked out to the big meadow. After a few minutes, Carl came out of the field grass.

Billy placed a few of the cookie drops in front of Carl. "I need some help from you," he said.

"You need what? Help from me?"

"Yes. When I met you, you had a terrible diet, and your breath was so bad it could have knocked over an elephant."

"Wait, wait! I changed my diet—"

"I know," said Billy, "but I want you to break your diet. I want you to go find something awful like that to eat, and then I want to take you for a ride in my backpack."

Carl lowered his eyes to ground level and looked around with a distant, dreamy look. "Hmmm. That sounds like *fun*. I used to *love* that stuff."

"Okay, then you do that, and I'll be back in an hour to pick you up."

"Yeah, well, okay, if that's ... wait, what's an hour?"

Billy jammed his hands in his pockets in frustration. *This was the problem with working with rats*, he thought. Then he got Carl to look at the sky, and he pointed toward the sun. He drew an arc with his finger from east to west, starting with the sun, a short arc in the sky. "That's an hour," he said. "That's fifteen degrees."

Below him, Carl said, "What's a degree?"

"Don't worry about it. When the sun gets to there"—he pointed to the spot at the end of arc again—"when the sun gets *there*, I'll be back."

And with that Billy turned and left the meadow. He heard Carl crawling back into the tall field grass.

Billy went home and pulled down his backpack. He hoped he could wash it out tonight when the day was done. He put a handful of cookie drops into a plastic bag and then read a few pages from a good book while the time passed.

When he got back to the meadow, he found Carl in the clearing with a sleepy smile on his face. "Wow, that was good," said Carl. "We should do this more often." And Billy could smell the awful stench on his breath, just from that. Billy turned his head away as he squatted down and helped Carl crawl into his backpack.

"How far we going?" he heard Carl ask. "Oh, not that far," said Billy.

Then he shouldered his backpack and set off across the big meadow toward the lane that would lead to the forest.

Drk Cha was waiting for him in the same spot they had met the day before. "I told you you're not welcome here," he said. He had a raccoon and a hissing snake with him, one on either side.

"And I told you to stay away from the black squirrels. Now, as you see, I have some very mean friends with me." And he gave Billy his most menacing scowl.

Billy said nothing. He lowered his backpack to the surface of the path and opened it to let Carl out. He whispered to Carl, "Now, you don't have anything to be afraid of. When I stand up, I want you to let out a huge breath, right at the big squirrel." And Billy stood up and turned back to the squirrel. Carl simply looked at the squirrel and the raccoon and the snake, and then exhaled a magnificent, tremendous breath.

The effect was electric. The raccoon squealed and then turned and trundled quickly off into the woods. The snake shook its head violently back and forth. It stuck its tongue out and then shook its head twice as violently. And then it actually slithered backward into the underbrush, and the snake, too, disappeared. Drk Cha waved his front paws furiously in front of his face and nose and closed his eyes in a squint.

Carl seemed to find this fun. He crawled closer to Drk Cha and unleashed another massive breath right into the white chest hair of the squirrel, who collapsed down into a low sitting position.

"Holy acorns, rat!" he said. "What have you been eating?" He looked up at Billy. "So what's your point, boy?" He swiped away in front of his nose again.

Billy answered calmly. "I think you and your gray squirrels have been acting selfishly and irresponsibly," he began. "The black squirrels need to forage, too. They didn't come this way to take over all of your woods. There's enough space here for all the squirrels to work together.

"Now, if I wanted to, I could get Carl the Rat to drive off you and all your gray squirrels for a huge distance, back deep into these woods. Your mean friends ran off the moment a problem came up. You aren't so smart, and you aren't so tough, but driving you off is not a good idea, either.

"I propose that you let the black squirrels forage up to *that* side of this path," he said, and he pointed to the side across from Drk Cha. "And the gray squirrels forage from your side to as far into the woods as you care to go."

"Aah, swamp water," said Drk Cha, with dismissive wave of his paw. Carl took in another deep breath, ready to let go again.

"But maybe we'll consider it."

Billy said, "I'll come back and check on things again in the winter, if that'll help."

"Yeah, you do that," said Drk Cha. "You go ahead and come back in the winter."

Billy paused, then reached into the vest of his thin jacket. "I brought a treat that might make this end in a more friendly way." He took out the bag of Magic-Be-Nice cookie drops. He put some on the ground in front of the squirrel. Drk Cha leaned down and gobbled up a cookie drop.

"Aah, who eats stuff like this?" He looked at Billy. "Where'd this come from?" he said.

"My mom makes those. They're special."

Drk Cha spit the rest of the drop out of his mouth. He turned and started to walk into the woods. All around him, Billy could hear the movements of hordes of squirrels in the branches and in the brush moving off in the same direction.

Drk Cha turned and looked back at Billy.

EPISODE 7

BILLY AND NEIL THE BEAVER

Billy Age 11

Billy stood waist-deep in the wide creek. He was just glad it had quit raining. It had rained for days, it seemed, but now the clouds had moved up the river valley. There they formed into a high, dark line, towering up into the gray sky.

Just up the creek from Billy was Neil the Beaver's dam. He heard a noise and looked over at the bank. There Neil stood where he had dragged a piece of wood to the bank. He dropped the branch in the creek, and it floated down to Billy. Billy took the branch and waded up to the base of Neil's dam. The beaver came out on the dam, and Billy handed the branch up to him. He and Neil made a great team.

As Neil moved the branch into place, he began looking up the river valley.

"What's up?" said Billy. His view was blocked by the dam.

"I hear a sound from upriver," said Neil. He turned back to his work, but then after a moment he looked back up the valley. He raised himself up as high as he could on his four legs. Suddenly, he swiveled back toward Billy and then back up the creek.

"Billy!" he said. "Run!" And he turned and waddled across the dam and back toward the bank.

Before Billy could make a move anywhere, he heard a loud noise like a freight train, and then the dam simply exploded over him. The water churned and raged and pushed him under. He felt pieces of the dam hitting him and, powerless before the flood, he was swept off his feet, tumbling in the swollen waters, rushing along the creek bed and headed now for the great river a mile downstream.

It was three weeks earlier, that day that Billy had decided to take a long afternoon walk. He had left the house where he lived with his mom, Betty Bumpkin. Taking small paths and a narrow dirt country lane, he walked first to the meadow with the great tree in the middle. He paused there long enough to scatter some poppy and fennel seed for the field mice. He sprinkled some Magic-Be-Nice crumbs for Carl the Rat. Then he headed across the meadow to another little country lane.

The lane took him in the direction of the deep woods, where little boys were told not to go. Billy felt a little older now so he thought he could head that way just a little farther than before. The lane twisted beneath a canopy of oak and poplar and maple trees. The weather was beautiful, the breeze was soft, and the sunlight dappled through the tree leaves onto the dusty lane. He heard the squirrels chattering away to each other in the branches.

He passed a gray squirrel standing on his haunches beside a black squirrel.

"Chatter! Chatter! Chatter!" they said.

He heard the birds singing, and they sang that all was well. He heard the scurry of other small creatures in the underbrush and in the ground cover of fallen leaves.

Other than for such sounds, the woods were sacredly quiet and peaceful.

The lane began to climb through some short, rolling hills and ended at a wide creek that Billy had never seen before. The water flowed sluggishly. A small path led along the bank of the creek to his left and his right. It looked like a path used by his friends, the deer and the fox. He decided to take the path to his left, so he walked that way, against the direction of the creek's flow.

After a while he came to a pond that looked like it must be a nice home for fish. Billy didn't know any fish, so he stood on the creek bank and watched for a few minutes. Soon he began to see brook trout through the water. They seemed sluggish, just like the creek's flow. He had heard that brook trout and bream would leap out of the water in astonishing jumps to gobble bugs on the surface. He didn't see any fish jumping.

Maybe it's just the wrong time of day, he thought.

A trout swam up near to him at the edge of the creek and looked up at Billy. So he squatted down and looked back at the fish and smiled. The fish waved his fins lightly to stay in place. His lower jaw moved slightly, and some air bubbles popped out.

"Blub! Blub!" Then he turned and swam indifferently away.

The creek narrowed farther up the valley. Billy followed on until he came to another pond. This one had a strange pile at the far end. As Billy drew closer, he realized that this must be a beaver lodge, although he had never run into one before. Extending out from the lodge, a crazy jumble of branches and twigs crossed all the way over to the near side where Billy was. He realized this must be some sort of dam. The water was shallow, so he waded across to get a closer look.

He found a path on the far side of the creek and followed it until he was just to the land side of the lodge. It was certainly a big structure. Beyond it he could see the dam, which struck him as a crazy structure. It was so crazy that he wasn't sure how it could hold back water, but it did. It backed up a pool of water above it. Now in *that* pond, he could see trout leaping. The bream were leaping, too.

Suddenly he felt a bump against his leg, which startled him. A beaver was pulling a skinny log after him about two inches in diameter and seven or eight feet long. The beaver dropped the log and squinted up at Billy. He stared long and hard.

"What're you?" he asked curiously.

"I'm a boy from the village," Billy said. "My name is Billy Bumpkin."

"Oh, yes, of course, of course, a boy from the village. You'll have to excuse me. My eyesight has been bad since I was a pup. My name is Neil. I live here."

"That's quite some home you have."

"Thank you. Yes, I like it very much, very much. Now if you'll excuse me, I wish to add this branch to the dam." Neil grabbed the piece of wood in his teeth and pulled it to the upriver side of his lodge. Then he carried and pushed it toward the far end of the dam where the current would hold it from floating off. He swam back to the bank beside the lodge, left the creek, and crept out over the top of his lodge to the dam. He walked out across the top of the dam to where he had left the branch. Reaching down, he grabbed it again in his teeth and hauled it up onto the dam. Then he came back to the lodge and onto the creek bank and headed back toward the woods.

"That's a lot of work," said Billy. "Is this what you do all day?"

"Well, I stay busy. After all, look at me—I *am* a *beaver*."

Billy thought. "What if I were to stand in the creek? You could float a branch out to me on the downriver side. Then you could go out on the dam, and I could hand it up to you."

Neil smiled and calmly shook his head, as if to say, "No, no, that's just not the way it's done." Then he seemed to think about it. He squinted up at Billy. He walked closer to the creek and stared out at the dam. Then he stared down at the creek, and then back at the dam. He walked back over to Billy.

"Well," he said, "I must say I've never seen it done that way, but I suppose it's worth a try." He waddled into the woods, and Billy waded out into the creek. Neil floated out a branch, and Billy handed it up to him when he was out on the dam. The system worked perfectly and saved Neil a lot of time and energy.

Billy liked Neil the Beaver, and Neil seemed to like Billy. So most afternoons for the next several weeks, Billy took the long walk through the meadow and past the great tree and along the lanes and up the path beside the creek until he came to Neil's lodge. They made good progress on the dam, and then the weather threatened to turn dark and ugly. One afternoon, Billy and Neil paused to take a break.

"I notice I never see any other beaver up here," said Billy. "Do you live out here alone?"

"Yes, yes, I've lived here alone for most of my life."

"Are you from here?"

"Of course. Beavers really don't like to travel all that much. And you see how long it takes to build one good dam and a solid lodge."

Billy listened quietly. He felt Neil had more to say.

"I was born here and raised by my mother. Now, my mom—she was a wonderful beaver mom."

"How come I've never met your mom?" asked Billy.

"Oh, she died."

Billy listened quietly, thinking again that Neil had more to say. And he did.

"Well, if you want to hear the story, it happened when I was just a pup. I remember the weather was bad, a lot like it looks today. I was swimming out there where you wade and I float the logs out to you. Silly pup games, like spinning around and trying to stand up on my tail to see above the water. Yes, yes. I suppose I was looking for fish. That would be crazy, because the fish live upriver of the dam, not on this downriver side. But what do you know when you're just a young pup?" He paused.

"And then suddenly the world caved in. I think in your village they would call it a *flash flood*. All I recall is being tumbled around and feeling I was going to drown for sure. I looked for the bank but couldn't see it."

He paused and looked at Billy with an uncomfortable little smile. "I don't have very good eyesight, you know.

"I could feel myself being washed down the creek, and I was helpless to save myself. Then when I had given up hope, suddenly I felt a big push against my chest and belly. I was pushed all the way over to the bank of the creek. I looked down, and it was my mom pushing me out of the flood. She got me over to the side, and I was just able to crawl out on some rocks. When I looked back for her, she was gone. I never saw her again."

Billy didn't know what to say. What if he were to ever lose his mom? Who would fix dinner? And who would be there to teach him all of the secrets of life and of the heart? Finally he said, "Gosh, that must have been awful."

Neil nodded. "Oh, yes. Yes, it was. It was—and will forever be—the worst day of my life."

After a few moments of silence, they went back to work on the dam. Just then the rain began to fall.

Billy tumbled and tossed in the furious current, pummeled by the flood's debris. Something had hit him hard on the nose. Another heavy object had rammed him powerfully between his shoulder blades and knocked a little more air from his lungs. He was at the end of his strength and at the end of his breath. He wasn't frightened. His adrenaline was running too high for that. No, most of what he felt was sadness. Sadness at going this way. In his mind, he saw Betty Bumpkin's face, and it seemed sad, too.

The water seemed to calm just a bit, and then he felt a sudden punch where the top of his stomach would be. And then he felt himself being pushed through the water, and his shoulder touched the river bottom, only the river suddenly seemed shallow. He reached down and felt a sleek, wet head. Then he felt the river's edge, and his head came out above the water. It was still raging fast. He reached above his head to the bank, and his hand found the bottom of a bush or a small tree. He realized he could pull himself from the river. He thought he might make it through this okay.

A sudden chill startled him to alertness. He had a quick memory of Neil's mother disappearing down the river. He slashed down with his free hand and just managed to grab a front shank, and he pulled himself, inch by inch, up the bank and out of the current, all the while desperately clinging to Neil. Neil felt lifeless and limp. Soon Billy could feel his heels dig into the bottom, and then a bit at a time—even while the water still raged and swirled around his legs—he dragged himself up onto the bank. He pulled Neil with him, and then the two of them lay stretched out across the pathway that ran high along the bank.

For a long time they just lay there. Then Billy found himself sitting up, staring blankly at the wild river. He felt Neil heave himself up behind him. For a moment, he just leaned his back against the beaver's shoulder. Then he stood up, and the two of them walked slowly back up the path toward the lodge.

The dam was gone. Not a stick remained. Billy was shocked to see the lodge still in place, and he supposed the water's rapid rush must have simply churned around it. Neil stared at the lodge too.

He paused and looked at Billy with his uncomfortable little smile. "You know," he said, "I guess they just don't build them anymore like they used to..."

Billy said, "Hang on a minute. I have something that might really help us right now." He found the little pack he had slung over his shoulder that morning. He reached into the pack and pulled out a bag with a couple of Magic-Be-Nice cookies inside.

"Here," he said, and he handed one to Neil. "My mom makes these, and they're special."

For a while that afternoon, the two of them talked about rebuilding the dam, which Neil would have to do because that's what beavers did. Billy suggested that they build it so that the trout and the bream downstream would have as nice a pond as the fish upstream had.

"You mean they never had that before?" Neil asked. Billy just shook his head. "Hmmm. I never saw things that way before," said Neil. And this made Billy smile his own warm smile, but inside and just to himself.

Late that afternoon, the river had calmed to the point where Billy could wade safely across. He and Neil agreed to meet the next day to begin the slow work of rebuilding the dam. And then Billy walked home.

EPISODE 8

BILLY BUMPKIN AND THE BIG BAD WOLF

Billy Age 11

Cold, clear sunlight fell through the Bumpkins' kitchen windows from a brilliant sky. "A young fellow like you," said Old Dave to Billy, "so many choices ahead of you in life. You have all the wonderful places to go. Just remember, boy, all of your choices have consequences, okay? Your mom just wants you to be careful."

Billy Bumpkin had a habit of wandering and exploring places. His mother, Betty, had talked with him about it. She had asked Old Dave, the wisest man in the village, to talk about it with him too. So he did. But Billy was at that age where he was sorting out what he had to listen to and what he really wanted to do.

Billy walked warily through the trees in the forest. He walked on pathways that were laid out more by the creatures of the forest than by men. He was in a place in the forest where he had never been before. He had not only explored into the deep woods that morning. This time, he had wandered so deep into the woods that he had reached a river. He crossed the river on an old bridge. Whenever people in the village and at the store brought up the subject of the river and the forest on the far side, conversation would die off. It was like adults were uncertain of what was over there.

Discussion of the far, far woods made them uncomfortable.

Billy walked and walked. He saw no one. He reached a hilltop that gave him a wide view of the woods. All around and ahead of him stretched nothing but trees as far as he could see. Forest paths wound here and there among the woods. He saw what looked like a large dog trotting along one of the paths. He watched it. The dog sniffed the air and looked around. Billy decided it would be best if he headed back toward the river. There was nothing more to see from up here.

After a bit of walking, he reached another hilltop. Along the way, he passed through mostly oak and pine and hickory. Tall and healthy and green. Beneath the canopy of the trees, the undergrowth was thick and tangled and strewn with thorny bushes. The cold, damp air tingled in his nose. That underbrush thinned out as he climbed to the next hilltop. He looked back and saw the dog on the hilltop he had left a while back. The dog saw Billy, too, and glared at him with yellow eyes.

Only it wasn't a dog. It was a wolf.

Upon seeing Billy, his lips pulled back into an ugly snarl, and he showed sharp teeth and dripping saliva. His brow curled down into a concentrated focus of fury. His head lowered with his shoulders as he gathered his rear legs to begin his chase. Billy watched with a growing sense of alarm and then realization. Then he did the only thing he could think to do.

He turned and ran as fast as he could toward the river.

The path he was following ran up and down low hills. It twisted and turned. The dirt was not muddy, but it was crumbly in places, and it was hard to run at top speed. He heard crashing in the underbrush behind him, and he tried to run even faster. Finally he saw the river. He burst out of the woods and came to the water. The river here was wide and the current ran swiftly. In no time at all, he heard a big crash behind him. He turned and found himself facing the crouching wolf.

Billy had never been truly scared for his life, but he was now. His knees felt weak and shaky. He glanced right and left, but he could see no route of escape. He turned back to the wolf.

The wolf snarled and growled. It was a blood-curdling sound. The snarl was deep and throaty and primitive. It froze Billy on the spot. The wolf kept snarling, and he lowered his front shoulders and gathered his hind legs under him for his charge. But then suddenly, the beast sat back and looked over each shoulder.

"Go!" he said to Billy in a low voice. "Cross the river— now!" Billy was stunned.

"Cross the river now!" said the wolf again, and with that he started to snarl even more fiercely than before.

Billy looked at the cold, swift river and pleaded with the wolf, "I can't swim across that. I'd drown!"

The wolf glanced back over each shoulder again. Then he trotted into the underbrush about fifteen feet to Billy's left. He seemed to be looking around. Then he trotted back across the trail, stopping in the middle to growl fiercely at Billy once more. He stalked into the scrub again, this time about fifteen feet to Billy's right. He came back and crouched again, right in front of Billy and this time closer. Again his voice came out low.

"Canoe. Over in the bushes. Get in. Cross the river. Now!"

Billy scampered into the brush and found the canoe. He saw a paddle in a shallow puddle in its bottom. Behind him the wolf began again to snarl and growl. Billy grabbed the front seat in the canoe and pulled with all his might. The canoe did not move. He glanced back toward the wolf. The beast growled sharply and charged forward two steps and crouched. Billy summoned all of his strength and dug his feet into the bank and leaned backward toward the river and pulled and pulled. With a start, the canoe broke free, and the bow plunged into the river. The sudden release made Billy fall back into the water.

The canoe started to slip past him, but Billy was able to hold on. In the shallow river's edge, he was able to swing his leg up and climb into the rocking craft. He scampered up and skipped into the rear seat. He picked up the paddle. Now, as he drifted into the swift current, he looked over at the wolf.

"Can I come back and help you?" he called out.

The wolf snarled louder than ever. He roared out across the water, "Never come back, boy! Never!"

Several days later, Billy walked out of his house with a bag of Betty's Magic-Be-Nice cookies. He had asked his mom for them so he could take one or two to a young boy named Jamie. Jamie did not know how to be at peace in the crook of a tree on a warm summer afternoon. He didn't know how to watch the mommy fox play with her pups, or how to feed the field mice. He knew how to sneak into peoples' root cellars and steal an ear of corn. He knew how to catch bream, and then pluck their eyes out with a hook to use for more bait.

Billy found Jamie laying a mousetrap at the foot of the great tree where Carl the Rat lived. Billy took the trap and tore the spring off and threw the pieces as far as he could in different directions.

"I thought you might be hungry," said Billy. He gave Jamie a Magic-Be-Nice cookie. "I have to go for a walk," he said. "When I get back, I want you to tell me if the mommy fox played with her pups this afternoon." And with that, he walked off toward the path that he knew led toward the far, far woods.

More than ever before, Billy could feel the quiet in the forest. He left the fields and meadows behind. He followed the solitary path that led toward the river and the old bridge. Several times he checked behind him, but nobody was there. The quiet felt comforting but sinister at the same time. And then he came to the foot of the old bridge. He set out across toward the other side.

He heard a voice behind him, "Billy!" He turned and saw Jamie at the foot of the bridge. "Can I come help you?" Jamie asked.

"No!" Billy called back, in as stern a voice as he could muster. "Get away from the bridge. It's not safe!" He walked toward the far side. He crossed the threshold of the bridge and looked for the nearest hilltop. It wasn't far away. He walked to the top and felt the breeze at his back, blowing ahead of him into the paths and the deep woods. The afternoon sun shined warmly on his face. He turned and saw Jamie had taken two or three steps onto the bridge and then stopped, just watching. Billy pointed at him, as if to say, "You hold it right there till I get back!"

Then he heard a noise, like a howl, deep in the far-off woods.

The wolf sniffed the air, his head tilted back and high. As the boy had hoped, the wolf caught Billy's scent and scanned the hilltops and found him. His face curled into a hideous snarl. His head lowered with his shoulders, and he gathered his hind legs beneath him. With a roar he charged toward Billy.

Billy turned and ran back downhill toward the bridge as fast as his legs would carry him. This was crazy, he thought as he ran, but there was some thought in his head that he had to resolve about the wolf. When he reached the bottom, he heard crashing noises, and he knew that the wolf had crested the hilltop. Man, that wolf is *fast*, he thought. He reached the threshold of the bridge and stopped, turning around. The wolf raced into the small clearing. He growled. He showed his huge canine teeth. Saliva dripped from his jaw. He lowered his head and shoulders. He gathered his legs behind him.

Billy stepped backward five steps onto the bridge. The wolf did not charge, but stayed in his crouch.

"I told you never to come back, boy!" he growled. "Now you've done it!"

"I thought you might be hungry," Billy said, and with that he hurled the bag with the rest of his mom's Magic-Be-Nice cookies over the wolf's head to the far side of the little clearing. The wolf stayed, crouched and ferocious, snarling at him. "Eat the cookies!" Billy pleaded. The wolf only growled louder. "Hey, you could come back, you know. To the other side," knowing as he said it that he sounded absurd.

"Can...Never...Come...Back! Stay...Away!" snarled the wolf, and now he unleashed his full, fearsome, almost mournful wolfish howl. With his jaws open, he seemed prepared to leap straight at Billy, and suddenly the boy knew how cold, primitive fear could quake in his soul. He backed up slowly on the bridge ten more steps. Then he turned and ran from the far woods for all he was worth.

The noise and the sight of the wolf had made Jamie back off the bridge onto the path. When Billy reached him, the younger boy's face was pale with shock and fear. Billy was panting for breath, and his heart was racing.

"What was that?" Jamie asked.

"Wolf," said Billy, still gasping for breath.

"Yeah, but…the wolf *talked* to you."

"I know. I was so scared…didn't know if I could throw the bag…C'mon, let's get the heck out of here." They ran most all of the way through the forest and to the meadows and finally back to Billy's house.

Two days later, Billy and his mom sat at the kitchen table with Old Dave. Once again, cold, clear sunlight fell onto the table.

Dave said, "Well, did you hear? Two fellows came into the town center last evening. They had the body of a great big wolf trussed up on a carrying pole and strapped on the hood of their truck. Said they seen him at the near side of the old bridge to the far woods. So they shot him dead." He paused. "Said he didn't even put up a fight. Said it was like he almost wanted to die. Or maybe he just wanted to come back over…" He looked at Billy, like he was waiting for the boy to say something.

"Mom, okay if I go out for a walk?"

"Sure, Billy, just be home in time for supper." Billy left, and as he did he saw Betty sitting wordlessly with Old Dave.

The first thing Billy did was walk into the town center. He saw Big Mike's truck parked at a new construction site. Then he walked to where the wolf was laid out on the ground, still bound to the carrying pole. He lay on his right side. His eyes were open and yellow, and his tongue lolled out of his mouth. His great canine teeth were bared, and his lips were curled back in a death-like grin. Billy gazed into the eyes and stared at the face. He remembered the panic he had felt when he had stared at that face, transfixed with fear that froze his muscles and limbs. He remembered the primal growl. He remembered the dripping saliva.

And he remembered the voice. *"Cross the river, now!"*

So what brought you back across?

He remembered tossing the bag of Magic-Be-Nice cookies into the clearing, then running back over the bridge.

You heard me, didn't you? he thought to the wolf.

He looked at the face again. He saw a savage animal, with hooked fangs and fierce, yellow eyes. He also saw, he thought, perhaps something else. Maybe a hint of a smile. Maybe something like acceptance.

So, how are you happier? Alive and ferocious in the far woods, or at peace over here like this? Are you back at home? He paused in his thoughts. *And, who are you? Or at least, who were you?* Who knew?

Billy looked back over his shoulders, left then right. No one was watching. He took his right hand and carefully reached out and closed the wolf's eyes.

Billy left the town center and walked out to the meadow where the field mice lived, along with Carl the Rat. He looked up and saw Jamie curled into a crook in the decades of branches in the great old tree. A cool breeze blew through the leaves. Sunlight dappled back and forth like little wavelets on the river.

"The little pups have been out playing with the mommy fox," said Jamie. "Actually, you know, it's kind of fun just to sit out here and watch sometimes."

"Yeah," said Billy, "I know. It is fun, isn't it? Yeah, it is. I know it is."

EPISODE 9

BILLY AND THE GREAT STORM

Billy, Age 12

The late summer storm was building in its unusual intensity in the sultry mid-day. Billy had left Old Dave's house to go home and see about his mom, Betty Bumpkin, against the advice and wishes of Old Dave himself.

"This has the looks of a twenty-year storm, boy," he said. "It's likely to get a lot worse before it gets better." And sure enough, Billy had not gone far along the familiar paths before he could feel much stronger winds buffeting his body and hard-driven rain stinging his face. He heard vicious gusts and even cracking branches and trees around him in the woods.

Then, coming around a bend in the path, he saw a tree that had been driven to its death stretched out across the path. And hiding beneath the bole of the tree, he saw his young friend, Jamie. The boy had his arms cradled over his head, and he was staring down at the path beneath him. Billy ran up to the boy and put his hand on Jamie's shoulder. Even as he ran, he had to shield his face against the hard rain.

"Jamie, are you okay?" He realized Jamie could not even hear him over the cacophony of the storm. "Hey! Hey! You okay?" he asked again, this time yelling as loud as he could. Jamie just looked up at him with a wild-eyed look. Billy realized that the young boy was simply terrified as the rain poured down on them in sheets.

"Come on! We gotta get out of here!" he yelled, but Jamie just stared down and shook his head violently. He cradled his arms over his head again.

Billy stood up and looked ahead up the path that led to the big meadow and then to his house. Even coming up from behind the fallen tree, he had to lean forward to maintain his balance. Just then, a brilliant flash of lightning struck, up near the meadow's edge, and instantaneously an explosion of thunder cracked over him. He looked up the path again, and then he looked back down the path toward Old Dave's house.

Billy was now about as tall as his mom. His work on the beaver dam and his chores around the house had begun to fill out his chest and arms with muscles. In one swift move, he reached down and grabbed Jamie at the front of his soaked shirt and yanked him to his feet. In the same move, he turned and hauled the younger boy—stumbling, screaming, and slapping at his hand—back down the path toward the house of Old Dave.

It seemed the only thing to do in a storm more ferocious than anything he had ever seen.

Earlier in the day, Billy had stopped in on Old Dave, and luckily had found him at home. Billy had something on his mind that he wanted to know.

Over the past year, he had found himself stopping in occasionally to sit and talk with the old man. Dave told him stories about the history of the town, and things about the other towns nearby and where Dave's family had come from in far-away New England.

This morning he had said to Old Dave, "I want to know who my father was."

Old Dave peered at him intently.

"I want to know who he was and what he did in his life and what happened to him."

Dave considered the question, and then he spoke. "I understand, Billy. But maybe I'm not the one who should answer these questions. Seems more like your mom would—"

"Every time we get near the subject, she gets quiet and sad, and then she just says that someday we'll have to talk about all that. I mean, I love Mom. I don't feel like I should push her. But I'm at a point…I'm like at a point where I just really want to know."

"But, Billy…"

"And I think you're a person she would trust to tell me what happened."

There was a fire burning softly in the fireplace, and Dave stood up and tossed another piece of wood onto the flames. He sat back down and looked at Billy.

"Fair enough," he finally said, and he looked Billy in the eyes. "Your dad was a man named Jack. I never met him. He and your mom met in a small city about a hundred miles from here. Everybody in the town, from what I hear, loved this man Jack. He and Betty decided to get married, and so they did. Neither one of them, it seems, had much family, so they just pledged their lives to each other.

"Jack taught history and math at the high school. He must have been a very good teacher, because one day he got a call to come interview for a teaching position in one of the state universities. Oh, he and your mom were both so excited about that.

"The interview was in a town across the state. Your dad got on a plane to fly over there." Dave was quiet for a moment. He seemed to collect his thoughts and emotions. "Something happened on the way over there. No one is really sure what. The season had gotten rough, and their flight took them over the mountains. The plane disappeared along the way."

Billy found himself staring into the fire. Now he knew, but now the truth was terrible to hear. "What about me?" he asked. "Was I born then?"

"Boy, this is hard, Billy," said Dave. After a moment, he continued.

"No, you weren't born yet. I've thought about it, and I doubt your mom even knew she was pregnant at the time. Best I can figure, you weren't born for probably another eight months." They were both quiet, but then Dave took back the lead in the conversation.

"Anyway, after you were born and the two of you were safe, I think Betty felt a need to move on. So she left that town, and she moved here with you." He got up to go the kitchen, but Billy kept on talking.

"Then, what about my father? What about this man, Jack? Where is he buried?"

The wind outside the house had begun to build to an eerie moan, a high and keening pitch. Billy and Dave could feel it shoving on the house.

Old Dave stopped and turned. "Plane crash is a cruel thing, boy. They didn't even find that wreckage until the spring thaw came to the high ranges." He paused again. Billy could feel the horror that was likely showing in his face. Dave continued.

"They identified maybe a few sets of remains. None of those was your dad. So, there was a service, but there never was what you could call a burial. The church gave Betty a Bible. Probably the one she still reads to you.

"So all she really came away with were her memories. And then, a few months later, she had you. And since then, you have been her life."

Thunder clapped sharply off in the hills. The wind picked up even louder, and they heard rain starting to smack on the windows.

"You okay, boy?"

Billy nodded his head woodenly, and said, "Thanks for telling me. I needed to know."

The brutal intensity of the storm was frightening. Billy pulled Jamie behind him, dragging him along down the pathway back toward Old Dave's house. Now the wind was howling from behind them, and it was tough for Billy to keep the two of them on their feet and moving. Brilliant bolts of lightning began to strike all around them. The thunder was everywhere and deafening and constant. In the hard winds, they heard trees crack and splinter and crash. Jamie had quit fighting, but he was sobbing and scared.

By the time they reached the house, both boys were drenched to the skin. Billy pulled Jamie up the porch steps and pounded on Dave's door until the old man opened it. He gave Billy a shocked look.

"What are you doing back here?" he asked. He shepherded the boys inside and slammed the door shut against the wind and rain.

"The path was blocked. There's trees falling all through the woods. And I found Jamie, scared half to death. All I could think was for us to get back to here." The boys were soaked through their clothes, and now they were starting to shiver. Billy looked at Jamie, and the boy's lips were slightly blue.

Old Dave pulled two chairs in front of the fire. The fire was sputtering smoke and sparks as gusts of wind roared down the flue. "You boys sit here," he said. He left the room and came back with two long flannel shirts.

"These will be a bit large, but they'll do. You boys stand up and strip off those shirts and then put these on and button them up." The shirts were indeed big, but they were blessedly dry. Billy's shirt reached to his knees and Jamie's almost to his ankles. Dave went on, "Now the pants, too. That's right, and the underwear too. We have to get you two dry." The boys stripped off the rest of their clothes and then huddled back down into their chairs.

The warmth of the fire felt like a miracle from heaven.

Dave bundled up the sopping clothes and took them to a back room. "When this is done, and if we still have power, we can dry those out pretty quick. I'm just not going to try messing with electrical switches in a storm like this." He looked out the window in the main room and stared off, listening to the moan of the winds and the snapping noises of the lightning and the thunder.

"This is some kind of major cyclone," he said, looking back out the window. "I'd bet those are near hurricane-force winds out there." He looked back at Billy. "I told you this was looking like a twenty-year storm? I'd say this may be a hundred-year storm."

Dave had a stove that ran off a tank of propane, and he made the two boys each a cup of hot chocolate. The chocolate and the heat from the fire began to make Billy almost sleepy. After a while, it felt as though the storm might be slackening.

Dave looked at Jamie and said, "And you, young fellow... What on earth were you doing out on a day like this?"

Jamie looked at Old Dave and then at Billy and then back at Dave. "I was doing what I've seen Billy do. He goes for long walks into the woods." He looked back at Billy. "And he knows things that nobody else knows." He now spoke directly to Billy. "And remember, I saw you talking to that wolf!"

Old Dave came around and looked closely at Billy. Then he looked into the fire and shook his head, and his face took on a smile of bemused wonder. "Boy, what have *you* been up to that we know nothing about...?"

Once the storm began to pass, it died off as quickly and meekly as it had roared to its ferocious peak. Billy said, "I need to get back and check on Mom. By any chance, did you dry those clothes yet?"

"No, but if you want to wait a half hour, I can—"

"No, I feel like I should go check on her and lend a hand, if she needs me. Okay if I just wear this shirt?"

"Sure."

Billy pulled on his shoes and his wet socks. They had dried a little by the fire, but they still felt cold and clammy and squishy. Well, they would have to do.

"I'll come with you," said Old Dave.

"Well, I have a better idea," said Billy. "I told Mom I was headed over here. My guess is that Jamie's mom has no idea where he is. And she's probably scared out of her mind. Maybe you could walk him home and make sure she's okay. Then, if you want, you could circle back by our house and meet us there."

Dave looked at him with his warm blue eyes. "Okay," he said. "Sounds good."

Billy went to the front door and started to open it. Then, on a thought, he turned to Dave and said, "Do you have a first aid kit? Just in case?"

"Probably a good idea too," said the old man, and he reached into his pantry and pulled out a small white box with a bright red cross on it. "Tell Betty I'll be there shortly."

Billy took the path that led up to the big meadow. He figured the lower path might be flooded at the stream. When he reached the meadow, he was astonished at the devastation. The field grass was all flattened. The great tree still had its decades of branches, but a number of them were snapped and hanging, and the tree was pretty well stripped of its foliage. Fallen trees lay stretched into the meadow. The tree where he had replaced the birds' nest was one of them. He hadn't given much thought to the animals at the height of the storm, but now he worried for them.

He ran across the meadow to the head of the path that led to home. It was slippery on the way down, and he had to step around uprooted undergrowth and tree branches. He kept a close grip on the first aid kit. It was weird moving around in the big flannel shirt.

When he reached his house, he saw that several trees were down, and there were no lights on in the house. One tree was down almost at the foot of stairs to the porch. Billy leaped over the tree and went up and knocked on the door and then went inside.

"Mom?" he called out. No answer. "Mom?" he called out again. "It's Billy, Mom."

After another pause, he heard her voice. "In here," she called from the kitchen. Billy moved quickly to the kitchen. The kitchen was almost as much a mess as the meadow had been. Something had burst through the window over the sink, and wind and rain must have roared into the room. Paper and broken dishes were scattered over the counters and floor. There were puddles and leaves and twigs all over the place.

Betty sat at the kitchen table with a cotton dish towel wrapped around her left arm. The dish towel was bloody. She was also bleeding from a cut on the left side of her head. Billy walked over to her. He looked closely at the side of her head and opened the first aid kit. He took out a gauze pad and a small bottle of alcohol and began to lightly dab at the cut. She winced and looked at his flannel shirt.

"Have you been at Dave's?" she asked.

"Yes, ma'am," he answered. "I was headed this way, but the storm suddenly got worse. There were fallen trees on the path, and lightning began to strike…"

"No, no," she said, "You did the right thing. Is Dave here?"

"No, he left to walk Jamie home."

She looked at him and said blankly, "Jamie?"

Billy smiled. "Long story. Can I see your arm?"

Betty unwrapped the cotton towel from her arm. There were several gashes, large and small, along her arm from her wrist to her shoulder. "Wow, Mom," said Billy. He used another pad to clean the cuts. He found some antibacterial ointment in the first aid kit and a roll of gauze bandage. He put the ointment on the gauze and then gently but firmly wrapped her arm, first from shoulder to elbow, and then separately from elbow to wrist. Betty looked at him work.

"Pretty good job!" she said when he was finished. About that time they heard Old Dave at the front door. He joined them in the kitchen.

"Wow," he said.

"The window blew out," she said. "It was crazy. I put my arm up…"

"Yeah, I can tell. Who wrapped this?"

She smiled. "Billy did!" Dave looked back up over his shoulder at Billy. Billy felt embarrassed and walked out the front door and out to the lane. He saw the old gray rabbit at the foot of the path up to the meadow.

"I came through the meadow," Billy said. "They really took a hit. I'm worried about them."

"They seem to be mostly okay," said the rabbit. He looked at Billy with his round black eyes. "They sent me to tell you. And they asked me to check on you, too."

"I guess I'm just glad we're all mostly okay. That was one scary storm."

"In all my years," said the rabbit, "that's the worst I've ever seen. But don't you worry. The meadow and its family will come back to life. It's just what happens when nature gets rough." And with that, and not another word, the rabbit turned and began to lope back up the path toward the meadow.

Lippety, lippety, lippety.

Billy walked back inside. Old Dave was sweeping the kitchen. Billy grabbed a small whisk broom and began to clean broken glass and paper off the kitchen counter. Dave left the kitchen and came back with a sheet and taped it up over the window with duct tape. Then he taped some cardboard over the sheet. They sat back down at the table with Betty.

"Jamie get back home okay?" Billy asked.

"Yep. You were right, though. His mom was scared silly. By the way, that's a nice job you did with the bandages on your mom's arm."

"He's becoming some kind of a special young man," smiled Betty.

"You're embarrassing me, Mom," said Billy.

Old Dave looked over at him. "Listen, boy," he said. "A man isn't a man just because he's full-grown or because he always knows the right thing to do. A man is the one who always wants to keep learning what the right thing to do is. And who takes action to help others. And who realizes that the learning never stops.

"As far as I can tell, boy, your mom is exactly right."

They were all quiet for a moment. Suddenly some lights came on, and they were all relieved.

"I think this would be a good time to make some Magic-Be-Nice cookies," said Betty.

And she walked to the refrigerator and got out some eggs and some butter. Then she reached into the pantry and pulled out some flour and some sugar. She walked all these ingredients to the counter, where all her special ingredients were lined up in the cabinet above. Then she paused just for a moment and looked at Billy and smiled. She went back to the pantry and pulled out a container of rolled oats.

Oh, boy, thought Billy, *oh, boy.* Because the cookies his mom made with the rolled oats in them were always her very, very best.

APPENDIX

BETTY'S RECIPE FOR MAGIC BE-NICE COOKIES

1½ cups flour

1 tsp. baking soda

½ tsp. ground cinnamon

¼ tsp. ground nutmeg

¼ tsp. salt

¾ cup butter, softened

¾ cup packed brown sugar

¾ cup granulated sugar

2 eggs

1 tsp. vanilla extract

1¾ cups rolled oats

2 cups raisins

Combine first five ingredients in bowl; set aside.

Beat butter and sugars in bowl. Beat in eggs and vanilla.

Beat in flour mixture until blended. Gradually add oats and raisins.

Betty puts a piece of parchment paper on a cookie sheet or cooking stone. She sprays the paper with a non-stick baking spray with flour. (Pillsbury makes a good one.)

Drop cookie mix by spoonfuls onto baking surface, 2" apart.

Bake at 375° F 10-12 minutes.

Cool on rack. Makes 4½ dozen.

(Much thanks to Dole Food Company for the heart of Betty's recipe.)